michael morpurgo

Lucky Button

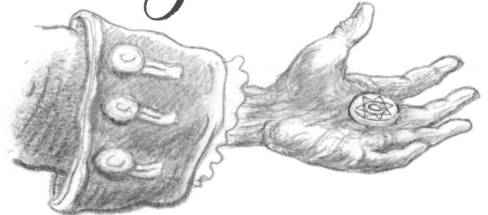

Illustrated by

Michael Foreman

WALKER
BOOKS

For Jeremy and Sarah
M.M.

To my artist hero William Hogarth, who supported
the Foundling Hospital, and Caro Howell and the
staff of the Foundling Museum, who have been so
helpful in the creation of this book.
M.F.

First published 2017 by Walker Books Ltd
87 Vauxhall Walk, London SE11 5HJ

2 4 6 8 10 9 7 5 3 1

Text © 2017 Michael Morpurgo
Illustrations © 2017 Michael Foreman

This book has been typeset in Sabon and Georgia
Printed in China

British Library Cataloguing in Publication Data: a catalogue record
for this book is available from the British Library.

ISBN 978-1-4063-7168-0 *(Hardback)*
ISBN 978-1-4063-8060-6 *(Paperback exclusive)*

www.walker.co.uk

CHAPTER ONE

The Two Worlds
of Jonah Trelawney

THE EIGHTH OF MAY. Jonah hated the eighth of
May. It was a date he wanted to forget, yet never
could. But he tried to that morning, as he got dressed
for school, took breakfast in bed to his mother as
usual, and settled her in her chair by the window, so
she could look out at her tulips in the garden. He gave
her a kiss goodbye. She smiled weakly and squeezed
his hand. It looked like it would be one of her silent
days. He was used to them.

Jonah gobbled down a bowl of cornflakes, shrugged

on his school bag, called out goodbye and left the house. At least he had the play rehearsal to look forward to, he thought. It could be a good day. But then a cyclist came past, and reminded him of what had happened on this day two years before. His mum had been riding her bicycle on the way to work at the library when the accident happened. The lorry had come too close, unbalanced her, knocked her off.

They had come to school that morning to tell him, to take him to the hospital. His mum had lain there for more than a week in a coma, her shallow breathing the only sign of life. She had woken one evening while he was at her bedside. She could talk, she could move everything in her upper body, but she was unable to walk. Ever since then she had been confined mostly to her wheelchair, her condition improving slowly, living through good days and bad days.

The long walk to and from school was always the best part of the day for Jonah. He looked forward to it, an untroubled haven between his two worlds: the world of school, and the home world he had just left behind at No. 3, The Cottages. Until the accident home had been a place of laughter and music. Not any more. As he shut the front gate behind him he turned to look back up at the house, at his bedroom window. The pigeon was there, strutting up and down on the windowsill. She was often there. She had shining purple feathers on her neck and Jonah thought she was very beautiful.

"Bye, Coocoo," he called out. "See you!"

It cheered him up every time he saw her. What he would give to be able to stay up there all day, sitting by the window and talking to Coocoo in the sanctuary of his room. There he could escape from it all – read, dream and listen to music on his headphones.

In his mind Jonah was up there now, looking out over the fields and woods to his other world of school, the roofs and chimneys just visible over the treetops in the distance. The upstairs of the house was all Jonah's domain now. Downstairs had been adapted for the wheelchair. On the good days his mum managed to walk with her frame or stick, but she couldn't manage the stairs.

As Jonah walked away, he hoped she might be feeling strong enough today to sit outside. Nothing lifted her spirits more. On days when the sun shone, like today, he knew his mum often ventured out to sit in the tiny garden at the back, among her beloved flowerpots. Jonah planted the tulip bulbs under her instructions every October, always red and yellow, and kept them weed-free and watered. Her tulips seemed to be her only real interest these days. She would spend much of winter in her chair, gazing out into the back garden, waiting, longing for them to grow.

Doctors and nurses and physiotherapists and health visitors came and went, sometimes when Jonah was there, but mostly when he was at school. They all told Jonah that the more he encouraged his mum to get out of her wheelchair and use her walking frame, the better. But that was all they said. How much of her disability was physical, how much was psychological, they seemed unwilling to discuss with him. His mum didn't like to talk about it, so he didn't ask. Jonah did all he could to help her with her physiotherapy exercises, which she hated, and to encourage her to play the piano again.

Before the accident, music had been his mum's chief joy. She never played or even listened to it now. Her beloved piano, that she used to play so much, remained closed and silent in the sitting room. The house had been empty of music ever since the eighth of May, two years before. The day the music died, as Jonah thought of it. There were many songs his mum used to play and sing. Jonah had grown up with her songs, had them in his head, hummed them, sang them.

He was humming the tune of "American Pie" now, one of her favourites, thinking about her as he walked along. He found himself looking at the photos of her on his phone: his mum sitting on her bike, and smiling and waving at him. And there was his favourite selfie of them both on the beach at St Ives eating ice creams, the summer before the accident. He found himself close to tears as he turned into the school lane.

Jonah cried often, but privately. It wasn't so much because he felt sorry for his mother, or himself. It was more out of anger, or from loneliness, or both. He had his own way of stopping the tears from coming, by singing, singing out loud, which was what he was doing now – a chorus from another of his mother's favourite songs, "Always Look on the Bright Side of Life".

He felt better already. It wasn't so bad. The two of them managed, didn't they? So she was a single mother, and he had never had a father. So what? They had each other. He had often wondered about the father he had never known. But you can't miss what you've never had. They did fine without him.

Jonah liked being with his mum. He liked caring for her; liked helping her in and out of bed; liked making their breakfast and supper; loved lying beside her on her bed every evening, after homework, watching television.

But there were those days when she seemed so low and miserable that she hardly spoke, and then nothing seemed to interest her, not Jonah, not the television, not Coocoo, not even the tulips. Occasionally she would be able to emerge from these dark times on her own, but Jonah knew she needed him more than anyone, that he was the only one who could help her chase away the shadows.

He discovered the best way to cheer her up was to sing to her. She might no longer listen to music or play the piano, but she loved listening to him sing her favourite songs. For her that was a source of great comfort and joy, a relief from the sadness that

sometimes felt as if it might overwhelm them. They
had become more than mother and son over these past
two years; certainly more than carer and patient. They
had forged a deep understanding, become the closest
and best of companions.

Jonah walked along, happier now, but reflective
still. Although he had never for a moment minded
having to care for his mother, he knew there had been
a price to pay for it. He often found himself very alone

in this other world he was walking towards. It was a loud world, of bustle and banter and babble, where he struggled to overcome his shyness, to fit in, to find friends.

He wasn't sure he had more than one friend in the whole school, and Valeria was hardly a proper friend – he just wished she was. Jonah had barely spoken to her. She was Russian and didn't speak much English; they communicated mostly in smiles. Smiles had to be enough, and they were. She at least seemed to be a kindred spirit, easy to be with. Jonah thought that might be because both were so often teased: Valeria for her accent, and because she had been new to the school that term; and Jonah because he was a loner.

Jonah wanted so much to make more friends, but it was impossible. He knew he could never spend time with them after school, or take part in any after-school activities. He would have liked to go with them on school trips, to theatres or museums, but that would usually mean coming home late, so he could never do it. He had to get home. His mum needed him.

More than anything, Jonah longed to be able to

sing in the school choir, as Valeria did. She played the clarinet too, like a dream. But choir and orchestra practice both happened after school hours. At least play rehearsals were in school time – that was something.

Even with Valeria, he was wary of mixing his two worlds. He found he could deal with each world better if he kept them apart. He never told anyone about why he had to hurry home after school, nor why he was late sometimes in the mornings. Most of the teachers knew his situation, and made allowances – though nothing was ever said – so he was never in any trouble over his lateness. They realized he was a carer, that his mother was alone at home and that Jonah had to look after her. But they were discreet, and rarely asked about her. That suited Jonah fine. His world of home was his business, and no one else's, and he would keep it that way.

CHAPTER TWO

Kill! Kill! Kill!

JONAH WASN'T AWARE OF IT, but he had been dawdling on the walk to school, taking his time even more than usual. He was always unwilling to get to school, and this morning there happened to be much to see on the way, much to divert him, much to dawdle over.

It was almost a clear morning, a few white puffy "Simpsons" clouds – as Jonah thought of them – against the deep blue of the sky. Across the fields he spotted a rust-brown deer grazing at the edge of the woods. She hadn't seen him. He stayed still, watching her. It was a bounding rabbit that disturbed her in the end. The deer sprang away, vanishing into the woods. The countryside seemed suddenly empty when she was gone.

But then the swallows were there, swooping down over his head, skimming the fields. The hedgerows all around were alive with birds: blackbirds, sparrows, chaffinches, wrens, and the pair of flitting goldfinches he so loved to see. The air was full of birdsong.

Jonah found himself singing out loud with them as he walked along the lane – this time it was "Here Comes the Sun". He knew every word, heard the accompaniment in his head. Yes, he thought as he sang, maybe this is going to be one of the good days. After all, the birds were singing, the sun was shining, and he had his play rehearsal first thing with Mrs Rainer to look forward to.

Mrs Rainer was far and away the best and most inspiring teacher he had. Everything about her was sharp: she had a sharp quick mind, sharp pointed shoes – always green – a sharp nose, and sharp darting eyes. And she was fair too, scrupulously inclusive. So in *Lord of the Flies*, the school play they were rehearsing, everyone had a part to play, though not necessarily the part they wanted. Mrs Rainer had created a musical adaptation of the book, and composed the songs herself. The pupils could help play the music, make scenery or costumes, or act in it. Valeria was almost the Pied Piper of the play. She played her clarinet on stage, drifting through and around the action, weaving the

story, making the magic, setting the tone and mood. She played quite beautifully.

Jonah loved to act. He came alive in the character of others, leaving all his shyness behind. He had wanted to play Ralph, the main – heroic – part, but even in the auditions, he'd known he wasn't right for the role. In the end Mrs Rainer had chosen him to play Piggy, and he was happy enough with that, proud of it too. It was a big part, important in the story. And he had the best song. Mrs Rainer told him that his singing voice was the main reason why she had given him the part.

Jonah liked the character of Piggy, empathized

with his bewilderment, his apartness, his longing to belong and his inability to do so. He didn't like what happened to Piggy in the end, of course, but he knew from school how cruel some people could be, and how right the author, William Golding, had been about the power of the mob.

No one was about as Jonah came wandering across the playing fields and through the iron gates. Every time he came into school, even though he'd been there nearly a year, Jonah was amazed at the sheer size and grandeur of it – especially after his little village junior school. There were acres and acres of playing fields and woods, and a wide gravel driveway that swept through wrought-iron gates and into a great courtyard with the school buildings all around. Impressive though it all was, Jonah found the place too huge, too austere, too stark. He loved only the chapel, which stood in the middle of the courtyard and had so often been his refuge from all the noise and clamour of the school, a sanctuary from the sadness of both his worlds. This was where he went when he wanted to be alone, when he needed to gather courage enough to face his worlds again.

The chapel, big enough to seat all seven hundred pupils, was just a small part of this great country house of a school, a place of towering chimneys, magnificent red-brick buildings and pillared cloisters. And this was a school with a story. Like everyone else, Jonah knew well enough what this place had once been, before it had become the local secondary school – they were all told its history by the headmaster at their very first school assembly, in the chapel. Jonah had never forgotten. His school had been built originally in 1935 to house the children from the Foundling Hospital in London, which was a kind of orphanage. For nearly

two centuries the lives of tens of thousands of poor and starving children had been saved by this Foundling Hospital in London. The children had been fed, cared for, educated, given a chance in life.

But as the years passed, the headmaster had told them, the city became too crowded and dirty for the foundling children. So this new school had been built out in the Hertfordshire countryside. Thousands more of these foundling children had lived here, in Jonah's school, boys in one half, girls in the other. They never mixed; they were hardly allowed even to speak with one another. They ate in one dining room – the dining room that was still used today – but in separate halves, at long tables and in silence, and they had to march everywhere, into the chapel, into meals.

Jonah made his way along the same wide echoing corridor where the foundling children had walked all those years ago, past the black and white photos of them on the walls, and imagined again how their lives must have been, this place their whole world, with no home to go to, no mother that they knew of, no father.

The school was quiet, Jonah thought, too quiet. Then he realized. Late, he was late again. Outside the rehearsal room he took a deep breath, dreading all eyes on him as he walked in, as he knew they would be. He knocked, went in, said sorry to Mrs Rainer, who waved him to his seat.

But then the ribald remarks came thick and fast. How often he wished his mother had chosen another name for him, and how he wished Jonah had not been swallowed by that wretched whale in the Bible. No one had made the connection until the headmaster had told everyone the story one day in assembly, so Jonah had him to thank for that. Once the story was out, there had been endless jokes on Facebook about it, about him, some of them so nasty it hurt. Almost overnight, his nickname at school had become Moby or Moby Dick.

"Evening, Moby," someone sneered as he sat down.

"Dickhead," said Marlon, so often his tormentor, and well cast as the bully Jack in *Lord of the Flies*.

To Jonah's complete surprise, Valeria turned on Marlon. Speaking very slowly and deliberately in her halting English, she said, "I think you should not say this. It is not good. It is not kind."

Her words fell on deaf ears.

"Blubber, blubber, blubber," came the whispering chorus all around the classroom. That was the name that really cut him to the quick, and shamed him. He had always tried so hard

to hide it, but they knew he cried easily. He felt the tears welling up, and tried desperately to hold them back, but he was failing.

Mrs Rainer saved him. She shut them up, withered them to silence. The tears were already in his throat, in his mouth too. He swallowed them, held himself steady, but all eyes were still on him. Marlon was smirking, waiting for him to crack. Jonah sang inside his head and kept the tears at bay, just. Suddenly the day was not going well at all.

But once the rehearsal began in earnest, he managed to ignore the jibes, become Piggy, and lose himself entirely in the story. He remembered his lines well, and Mrs Rainer made no secret of the fact that she liked the wholehearted way he was playing his part. He did worry, when the time came to sing his "Home again" song, whether his voice would hold, but somehow it did. He was singing it not as Jonah but as Piggy, and Piggy was singing loud and strong, and in tune. "Home again," he sang. "When will I be home again?" Mrs Rainer was nodding her approval all the way through, and best of all he could see Valeria was enjoying the song, willing him to do well, and then, when he had finished, miming a little clap for him.

Now came the moment of high drama in the play, when the others turned on Piggy to attack and kill him. Mrs Rainer was at the piano. She had turned the murder almost into a ballet: for greater impact, she said. And it worked. Everyone had to slow their movements right down as they gathered round Piggy for the slow-motion kill. "Kill! Kill! Kill!" came the rhythmic chant, their feet stomping in time, building slowly to a thunderous crescendo.

But in among the chanting Jonah began to hear something else, a different chant, not rehearsed, not in the play at all. "Blubber! Blubber! Blubber!" He realized that all the slow-motion pretending, the simulated violence, was becoming real. It was Jonah they were attacking, not Piggy at all. This was personal now. He caught a glimpse of Marlon's face, saw the venom in his eyes, his face twisted, grinning. Marlon wasn't acting. He was enjoying it too much. The punching and the kicking might still be feigned, but they were meant. Now Marlon was kneeling on

top of him, hand on the back of Jonah's head, pushing his face into the floor. Jonah tried to squirm away, to curl himself into a ball, to protect his body, his face, his head. "Blubber! Blubber! Blubber!" came the chant again, Marlon's voice loud in his ear.

Suddenly the chanting stopped, and Marlon was off his back. Jonah dared look up. Mrs Rainer was pulling Marlon away by the scruff of his shirt. Then she was crouching over him. "Are you all right, Jonah?" she asked. "Are you all right?" Above him, there was a crowd of faces looking down at him, breathing hard, all silent now.

"Just making it real, Miss," Marlon protested. "You said we had to mean it, Miss. Mean it when you act. You said."

Jonah could feel blood warm on his lip, dripping from his nose. Mrs Rainer helped him up onto his feet. Valeria was offering him her handkerchief, putting it to his face, making him hold it.

"You should be ashamed of yourselves! Sit down immediately, the lot of you!" Mrs Rainer did not hide her anger. "And not a word while I'm gone. I'm taking Jonah to see the nurse. Not a word! You hear me?"

The school nurse sat him in her room and told him to

pinch his nose. She kept asking if he was feeling all right. Jonah nodded. He couldn't speak. He wouldn't speak. He just wanted to get out of this place and never come back. When the nurse was called away, Jonah grabbed his chance. He ran for it, taking the stairs in twos, and raced along the corridor to the front entrance. He wanted to go home, but knew how upset his mother would be. He had to give himself time to calm down, to stop his nose bleeding, before he could face her. She mustn't see him like this. It would distress her too much.

"Nice day?" she would ask him. It was always the first thing she said when he got home.

"Fine, Mum," he would reply, because he always did, because he couldn't worry her, could never bring his troubles home. She could not cope with him being unhappy – he knew that. He had to be strong for her.

Jonah made for the chapel, the best place – the only place – to be alone, to have time to recover. He hoped it would be empty.

CHAPTER THREE

The Phantom Organist

THE LATCH WAS HEAVY; the door creaked open. No one was inside. How many hundreds of those Foundling Hospital children had come to cry in this place, just like I am now, Jonah wondered. Ever since he had heard about them, he had identified with those children, imagining them to be as lonely as him, and he felt a strong connection with them, so much so that he had wondered more than once if perhaps he had even been one in a former life. Sometimes, alone in the chapel, he would break into one of his mum's songs, sing it to the foundling children who were there, he felt, listening. They had sung in this place; this was where they had come to sing their hymns and say their prayers twice a day, three times on Sundays.

He made his way to his usual spot, an aisle seat in the pew halfway down, on the boys' side of the chapel, the right-hand side – he knew they'd sat there from one of those photographs in the corridor. He sat down, closed his eyes, and became one of those children. Here he could cry with them, speak to them, tell them his troubles, as he had done so often before. Now he could let all his pent-up tears flow freely. He kicked out, stamped his feet and shouted out loud, the whole chapel echoing with his anger. When he had finished and there were no more tears left, he sat there, fists clenched, breathing heavily. The children had been listening, had heard him silently. Every one of them knew how he felt, he was quite sure of it. Emptied of all his pain and anger, he was numb now, his cheeks wet with crying, his nose throbbing. The blood was still trickling. He could taste it. It tasted strange, of metal and of silence. He held Valeria's handkerchief to his nose.

She had been so kind, and brave too. He was looking down at the bloodied handkerchief in his hand, when he noticed something glinting on the floor by his feet. He bent down to pick it up. It was cold and heavy in his palm, a button of some kind, a gold button. He

held it up to the light. He looked at it more closely, and saw that it was embossed with a shining star.

At that moment, out of the silence of the chapel an organ began to play, softly, from above and behind him, sweet and gentle at first, then the notes gathering upon one another into great thunderous chords that filled the chapel, filled his ears. Jonah had never in his life heard such an overwhelmingly wonderful sound.

He let it flow into him, into his ears, down his neck and his back, felt his whole body basking in the beauty of it. He was warmed through from the roots of his hair to the soles of his feet.

But something was puzzling him, worrying him. He had never before heard the organ playing in the school chapel. No one had played it for years; he was sure that was what he had been told. He had assumed the organ was defunct. They used the piano at the front of the chapel for assemblies sometimes, but never the organ.

And then he remembered the story Marlon had told him – a silly ghost story, just to frighten him, Jonah had thought – about how some people had heard the organ playing before they came into the chapel, and how it always stopped the moment the door was opened. No one had ever seen this phantom organist. But who else could have been playing the organ? Jonah was sure he could hear it. He was not imagining it. A cold shiver of fear crept up his spine and prickled the hair on the back of his neck.

Then Jonah had another thought. They must have

heard every word he had been shouting, must have heard him crying. He certainly did not want to have to explain himself to this organist, whoever he or she was, phantom or not. So, slipping the gold button into his pocket, he stood up and began to make his way as noiselessly as possible towards the door. The organ was still playing; but it was a different melody now, a different rhythm, more melodious, softer altogether, a tune he recognized at once: "American Pie". There could be no doubt about it. Then the key, the rhythm, the volume, the tune, changed again, and became "Always Look on the Bright Side of Life". His mum's songs: his songs!

He had almost reached the door now, but was somehow reluctant to leave, despite the hair standing up on the back of his neck, and the crescendo of fear gathering inside him. Scared out of his wits though he was, he still hesitated, his hand on the latch. How could this person know these were his tunes, his mother's tunes? Or was it simply a coincidence? No, it couldn't be. He didn't dare turn round, or look up to where the organist must be sitting. He longed to know who it was up there. But fear had its grip on him. He had to get out of there. Now.

The very moment he lifted the latch the music stopped.

"Wait! Do not go yet!" It was a commanding voice, a man's voice. "I shall be down just as quickly as these old legs can carry me, Master Trelawney."

Whoever it was knew him by name! Footsteps were coming slowly down the staircase now from the organ loft. The organist, still invisible, was talking as he came. Jonah could see no one in the darkness at the back of the chapel.

"I have oftentimes heard you singing those songs when you come in here, and I confess I have heard you crying too, and listened to your tales of sadness. How is your mother today, by the way? In better health, I trust."

A figure appeared now out of the shadows, a tall man, tottering, leaning heavily on a cane as he approached. He wore a long coat with buttons, buckled shoes on his feet, and a wig – a long, curling, rather grubby-

looking wig – down to his shoulders. Jonah wanted to turn and run, but his feet seemed rooted to the spot. He could not move. He could not speak.

"Do not gape so, Master Trelawney," came the voice again. "This is how we all looked in my day. And in my day it was not thought polite for a child to stare at his elders."

He was walking slowly, very slowly, down the aisle. Every step seemed to be an effort. He sat down heavily in one of the pews, clearly relieved to take the weight off his feet. Jonah was still transfixed with fear.

"You have found my button, I think," he said. "It is very precious to me. You will see from the star on it that it is a button from the uniform of the Coldstream Guards. Not gold, more's the pity. Only brass, but precious to me all the same." He held out his open hand towards Jonah. "I am most grateful you found it, but may I have it back now, please?"

Jonah's instinct was to open the door and run, fast. But still his legs would not move, and his mouth would not speak.

"Come, Master Trelawney, sit yourself down here. I do not bite. I would not harm you. I am a ghost, a phantom, as I think you must have guessed by now, but not at all the kind of spirit you should fear. And I would very much like to have my button back. That button is most important to me, more important than you know."

Jonah found himself walking back down the aisle towards him, but not because he wanted to. It was as if he had no will of his own. He was moving in a trance, being drawn in closer and closer. His legs were walking, without his ever intending them to, his eyes never once leaving the old man's face. Then he was sitting down behind him, not too close, open-mouthed, wide-eyed with fear.

"My button, Master Trelawney," the old man said, still holding out his hand. "You have it in your pocket, I think."

Jonah could not remember which pocket it was. He pulled out the bloodied handkerchief first, then felt the button inside it.

"You are most kind," said the old man, as Jonah
passed it over. He turned it over in the palm of his
hand. "I had looked everywhere for it. It is a part of
me, this button, a part of who I am."

The old man, Jonah could see now, was even older than he had first imagined him to be, his face creased and lined, his eyes deep-set and dark, his cheeks hollow. The eyes, a deep blue, brightened suddenly as he broke into a smile.

"Well, Jonah," he said, "have you looked your fill? I am not a pretty sight, I know. Age tells its tale, and I am a very great age, Jonah, over two hundred and fifty years old – I long ago stopped counting the years. So yes, I am indeed a ghost. But do not let that concern you. I haunt, but only with good intent, I assure you. I am

here because I like hearing children's voices. I love to hear them sing. And I love to hear you too, Jonah. I wish you no harm, believe me. I am a spirit, most certainly I am, but I seek out only kindred spirits, and I believe I have found one in you. I know you better than you think. Every time you have come in here and sung your songs – and in truth you sing wonderfully well, with a perfect pitch and most exquisite tone – I have been listening. I have heard your sorrows, Jonah, witnessed your tears. I think I know you as well as any man, alive or not – better even, I dare to say, than your own mother."

From somewhere Jonah found at last the courage and the voice to speak. "Who are you?" he asked in a whisper.

"I shall tell you soon enough," the old man replied, turning the button over in his hand and then showing it to Jonah. "You see the star? It has shone for me and it will shine for you. It is good to have it back. Thank you again kindly for finding it. I am glad you did, for it has given me the opportunity to speak with you. I have long wanted to do so. You and I, we have more

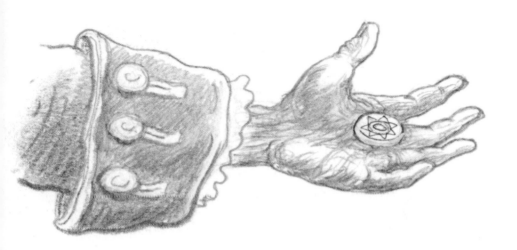

in common than you could possibly imagine. Our lives may be hundreds of years apart, but they meet here today, and all because of this lucky button."

"Lucky button? Why lucky? I don't understand."

"You will soon enough, Master Trelawney," said the ghost. "Once you know my story, you will."

CHAPTER FOUR

Lucky Button

LEANING TOWARDS JONAH, the old man said, "How does this stranger know my name? Is this what you are wondering? Well, I drift around, as ghosts are wont to do. I keep my eyes open, my ears open, my heart open too. I know you well. You come often into my chapel, do you not?" Jonah could only nod. "And what think you of my organ-playing, Jonah?" the old man went on. "Have I lost my touch? How well do I play?"

He did not wait for an answer. "I learnt my music-making from a master, you know, and he was the best friend I ever had. Without him, I would never have found myself – we all have to find ourselves, Jonah, or life is not worth the living – and what is more, without him I would never have found this lucky button. And this lucky button found you, and brought us together at last. Here, hold it again, while I tell you why I have so longed to meet you and talk to you. Now that you have picked up my button, I can speak with you at last."

On he went with scarcely a pause for breath. "Like you, Jonah, I was often alone as a child, much weighed down by sorrow and care. I have heard you opening your heart in this place. For almost a year now I have listened to your story, to your prayers, your cries for help. I have heard your songs too. And I know why you sing: you sing to bring yourself comfort and joy, do you not? To banish those bitter tears inside you. Singing, music, did the same for me. It still does. I know the taste of those tears. Like you I often felt alone in this world, for I was a foundling, a child given up by my mother. I should have died in a gutter or ditch somewhere had it not been for one man. We can change our world for the better – it is what we are here for – and this man did just that. Thomas Coram was his name, a shipbuilder and mariner who, seeing the misery of the poorest of children begging and thieving and dying in their infancy in the squalor of the streets

of London, decided that something must be done to save them.

"It took him nearly twenty years to find the money he needed – he was not a rich man, this Thomas Coram. But he made friends among the great and the good, touched their hearts, pricked their consciences, and wheedled the money out of their pockets. In time he had the wherewithal to build his Foundling Hospital, a refuge from the starvation and poverty and disease of London, and a school for foundlings such as me.

"It was to this place that I was brought in the cold of winter, a seven-week-old infant, and handed over on the doorstep, with a note that gave only my name, my date of birth, and the name and address of my mother. Along with the note came this button, the very button in your hand, Jonah, a token left by my mother to identify that I was indeed her child, should she ever come back to find me and claim me. Of course, I knew none of this as that little seven-week-old child, mewing in misery, blue with cold, and at death's door itself."

Jonah was still trying to take it all in, the brass button in his hand, this strange ghostly presence from the past sitting there talking to him. He was trying to understand whether this was all really happening, and not some kind of dream. He clutched the button tight, so hard that it hurt. The button bit into his hand. The button was real. This was all real; this was happening.

The old man reached out and put a hand on his arm. "Are you listening, Jonah?"

Jonah was trying to work it all out. "So you were one of those foundling kids?" he ventured.

"I was indeed, a year or two ago now, of course, or rather a century or two." The old man chuckled. "It was when the Foundling Hospital was in London, before they moved away and built this place instead. In truth I have no memory of being left there as a babe. Memory, for good or ill, does not reach back to our earliest moments of life. I do know now that they gave me a new name, Nathaniel Hogarth, Nat they called me, and I do know that all foundlings, such as I was, were given into the care of a wet nurse, a foster mother, often living far out in the countryside, away from the stench and decay and disease of London. And so it was with me.

"I grew up in Paradise, Jonah," he went on. "That was the name of the cottage that became my home – Paradise Cottage, so near the sea that I could hear the murmur of it all the while, smell the salt in the wind. I grew up healthy and strong, far from the foul stench of the city streets. I was looked after by my foster mother – I called her Mrs Ma – who lavished all the love and care upon me that I could ever have wished for, as did her husband, whom I called Mr Pa. I was a much-treasured child who became the heart and soul of a home that rang with laughter. I wanted for nothing. To them I was 'our dear little Nat' or, more commonly, 'our lovely boysie'.

"My memories of my time with Mr Pa and Mrs Ma are full of delights: butterflies and flowers in the garden; digging potatoes; Mrs Ma's wondrously delicious tattie pie; riding home from harvest fields with Mr Pa on Friend, the big farm horse; paddling in the sea and swimming in the dykes. Unlike most children, Jonah,

I became a strong swimmer very young. Mr Pa taught me much: how to swim, how to tickle a trout, how to pick out a horse's hoof; and Mrs Ma told me stories and sang me to sleep at night. My love for singing I learnt from her; my love for living from both of them. For a foundling child, for any child, this was a true paradise."

The door of the chapel opened suddenly. It was Mrs Rainer.

"They told me you might be here," she said, walking towards him. She seemed to be paying no attention to the old man, which was strange, Jonah thought.

"Are you all right?" she asked, crouching down beside him and putting a hand on his. "I thought I heard voices, a man's voice." She was peering over his shoulder. "Are you alone in here?"

That was when Jonah looked around and saw that the old man was gone. He wondered again for a moment whether he had imagined the whole thing. But then he felt the button in his fist. He opened his fingers. It was still there, in the palm of his hand.

"What's that you have?" she asked.

Jonah thought quickly. "Nothing, Miss," he told her, closing his fingers around it quickly. "Just a button, that's all. I always have it. It's lucky."

"How is your nose?" she asked, lifting his chin. "Stopped bleeding? Better now?" He nodded. "You want to come back to rehearsal, or stay here for a bit? Do whichever you like. If you want to be alone for a while, I quite understand." She looked around the chapel. "It's full of spirits this place, I always think – you know, of those foundling children. Poor souls." She brushed his hair off his forehead. "What happened back there in rehearsal, Jonah – I'm truly sorry. And they are too, all of them, I promise you. I don't know what came over them."

"Can I stay, Miss, for a while?" Jonah asked.

"Of course," she said, standing up. "I'll tell the nurse you are all right. She was worried. Take as long as you like; come back when you feel you can. We can't do this show without you, you know."

And then she left, closing the door behind her.

Jonah somehow knew the old man would be back in the pew even before he looked round. He was sitting exactly where he had been before.

"I am seen only when I wish to be seen, and only by those whom I choose to see me," he said, smiling. "I have much still to tell you. She seems to be a kindly soul, Jonah, your Mrs Rainer, but I do not care for her shoes. Too pointed. Now, where was I?"

"Mr Pa was teaching you how to swim," Jonah told him.

"You listen well, Master Trelawney," the old man said. "The truth is, I remember not nearly enough of my foster parents, only that I was loved, that they made me a happy child. But they could not protect me from the world. One day – I would have been about four or five, I do not recall exactly – Mrs Ma took me suddenly off to London. The journey was an adventure for me. I had never been on a coach, never been away from home. Until then the village and that cottage had been my world. I did not know why I was going, nor what I was going to, until we arrived at the gates of the Foundling Hospital.

That parting was my first great sorrow. I remember the pain of it to this day. I can see Mrs Ma walking away from me even now.

"They dressed me in different clothes, the same brown uniform all the other boys wore. They gave me a number which I was told was to be worn always on a string round my neck. I was no longer 'our dear little Nat' or 'our lovely boysie'. I was now Master Nathaniel Hogarth, number 762 of the Foundling Hospital.

"Our lessons were long and often tedious, our nights cold and lonely. They punished us frequently, the matron more than anyone else, with the cat-o'-nine-tails on our hands or the back of our legs. How we hated and feared her. We slept in lines, marched in lines wherever we went. Everything was inspected,

our hands, our hair, our clothes, and our masters were strict with us, their voices hard-edged. There was little gentleness, little kindness, in this place.

"Here, for the first time, I realized I had been born a foundling like all the others. I was reminded again and again by the matron when she was reprimanding me, telling me that I should understand how fortunate I was, that I had no home but this school, that I belonged nowhere. She it was who told me that Mrs Ma and Mr Pa were not my mother and father as I had supposed them to be. I had no father and mother. None of us did. We were entirely alone in the world."

For a moment he seemed overwhelmed by the sadness of his memories, and unable to go on. When he did, Jonah saw the tears in his eyes, heard them in his voice.

"I cried as you do, Jonah," he went on. "And where did I escape to do my crying? To the chapel, as you do – and it was very like this chapel too. It was the only place I could be alone. How I longed to be 'our lovely boysie' again, to see my dear Mrs Ma and Mr Pa, to swim again in the dykes, to ride on Friend, to watch the hares boxing in the fields, and to hear the skylarks singing.

"But do not imagine I was always unhappy. I did have happy times too in this Foundling Hospital. We had each other. We were a band of foundlings. We may have been, all of us, alone in the world, but we were bound together by this circumstance, and there is real solace and companionship in that.

"And there was fame too. Foundlings we might have been, but we soon learnt we were a source of great curiosity to those living outside our walls. From time to time, the rich and the great in society would come to stare at us. We were, one of the elegant ladies who often came visiting told me, the most famous foundlings in the land. Once, even the king came, King George. For him, and for all these lords and ladies in their grand clothes, we always had to behave perfectly, look smart, stand up straight, have clean hands and fingernails, remember how fortunate we were, and, most of all, we were told, we had to look happy.

"It was never easy to look happy, I discovered, when I wasn't. Every day, every night, of my life I missed Mrs Ma and Mr Pa. I longed for them and for my home in Paradise. We lived so much in enforced silence. At meals no one was allowed to speak. In class no one spoke, unless to answer a question. In our dormitories at night we never spoke. If we did, and if we ever dared to speak to the girls who lived in the other half of the school, Matron's punishment was immediate and severe. There were times when, even with my friends all around me, I felt quite alone in this world.

"But I thank God that I had one great and comforting joy: music. So you see, Jonah, you and I, we share some of the same sadnesses, and the same great joy. Music was my friend, the best friend I had. I think you know what I mean, Jonah, do you not?"

CHAPTER FIVE

Hot Pies and Roasted Chestnuts

THE SCHOOL BELL WENT THEN, distantly, but jangling and insistent as always. Jonah winced at the sound, its shrill electronic pitch, the urgency of it.

"I too never liked the school bell," said the old man, "though ours sounded rather different, of course. I would go around the school ringing it sometimes; we all took our turn. Church bells I loved and still do, but a school bell was never music to my ears. I loved all other music, Mrs Ma's greatest gift to me. She first sang to me as I sat on her knee, first played her fiddle to me in the kitchen at home. Dear Mrs Ma, she it was who first told me I could sing like an angel, who first sowed the seed of my love of music."

The school bell stopped. The old man smiled. "That's better. Now, where was I?"

He answered himself. "Ah yes, dear Mrs Ma," he went on. "If Mrs Ma sowed the seed, then Mr Montefiore grew it and helped it bloom."

"Who was Mr Montefiore?" Jonah asked.

"Our choirmaster at the Foundling Hospital, and quite the kindliest master in the whole school. Because of him, I found myself singing every morning of my school life in the chapel services, and every Sunday evening too. And Mr Montefiore it was who so often chose me to sing solo before the whole school, and to perform for those lords and ladies when they came to visit, to gawp at us, to see for themselves what foundling children looked like. I sang for them, always fiercely determined that they should see and understand that we were not mere objects of their pity and charity, but could sing as well as any other children – better even, maybe.

"Then one happy day the greatest composer of our age, George Frideric Handel, already an old man by this time, came to the Foundling Hospital and heard us singing in the chapel. I had no idea he was there in the congregation, but he came afterwards to the vestry and told me in front of Mr Montefiore and the whole choir that he should like me to sing in his oratorio the *Messiah*, which we all knew he conducted and performed with an orchestra and chorus every Christmas time in our chapel. It was performed only for the great and good, not for little foundlings like us, so we had never been there to see it. But we had heard them rehearsing, seen everyone arriving in their carriages, all in their finery. Can you imagine how I felt, Jonah? Me, Nathaniel Hogarth, foundling child number 762, singing for Mr Handel in his sublime *Messiah*, and in front of all those people!

"Mr Montefiore seemed struck dumb in the presence of this great man, but I was not. The courage

of youth, maybe. I told Mr Handel, to his face, that I would be honoured to sing for him. I had no fear of him. He might have been the most famous composer in the land, but I was not in awe of that. He had a kind face, gentle watery eyes like Mr Pa, and he was asking me to sing. I loved to sing. What was there to fear?

"Nor was I the least fearful in rehearsals in front of others, or when I sang some weeks later before the hundreds of people assembled there in the school chapel to hear us perform Handel's great *Messiah*. I imagined I was singing back in my childhood home, back in Paradise Cottage, with Mrs Ma and Mr Pa. In my head I sang my part in the *Messiah* for them, and for Mr Montefiore, and for Mr Handel, our much-loved composer and conductor too. Very old he might have been, and stooped with age, but he was always resplendent and elegant with a wondrously tumbling wig. I did not know then that every time we sang Handel's *Messiah* in our chapel he gave all the money he made from the performances to the Foundling Hospital. He was a good man with a kind and generous heart for those less fortunate than himself."

Jonah had been struggling to remember, and now he did. "I think I know the *Messiah*!" he told the old man. "My mum used to play tunes from it on her piano, at Christmas. She cried sometimes as she played, because it was so beautiful, she said. But she doesn't play her piano any more."

"Your mother is right, Jonah," the old man said. "Handel's *Messiah* is indeed gloriously beautiful, quite sublime. Such music touches the heart, stirs the soul. To sing in it every Christmas, as I did as a child, was the best thing that ever happened to me in that place; gave me the strength to persevere, to survive the rest." The old man took a deep breath and sighed. "But it could not last. The great and beloved Mr Handel passed away, and a couple of years afterwards the time came for me to leave the Foundling Hospital. They took me away from my music, from my singing. We knew this moment would come for each of us, the time to go out into the world and be apprenticed to some trade. Some went to be joiners or masons, some into domestic service; some became soldiers or sailors. I wanted only to be a musician. I wanted to learn to play in a band, in an orchestra, be a fiddle player, perhaps, or a drummer boy. Nothing else interested me. But the truth was that none of us had much of a choice in the matter.

"Mr Montefiore did his best to find a place for me, which indeed he did, but not as a musician as I had hoped. I was to be an apprentice at the house of a good friend of his in Chiswick, one William Hogarth, a painter, but also, Mr Montefiore assured me, a man who had a good and kind heart, who had devoted his life and his art for the benefit of the poor and needy. Hogarth worked tirelessly for the care of the children who came to the Foundling Hospital. He was a great man, Mr Montefiore told me, who would do all he could for me. I would have to make the best of it.

"I was filled with sadness at this news. Life at the Foundling Hospital might have been hard, but it had been my home all these years, and the other boys the best of companions. Like brothers together we had been. So it cheered me somewhat when Mr Montefiore told me there would be music in the house where I was going, concerts and recitals. He had played there himself, he told me. All had been arranged; Mr Hogarth would be my master now, and I would be working in the stables with his horses. I knew and liked horses, of course, from my days with Friend and Mr Pa at Paradise in my early childhood, you remember?" He paused and leant towards me. "Why do you frown at me so, Master Trelawney?"

"There's something I don't understand," Jonah replied. "Hogarth? That's your name too, isn't it? Nathaniel Hogarth, you said."

"You listen well, Master Trelawney," he said, nodding his approval. "And it is true, as you say, that my new master and I shared the very same surname, and I was soon to discover why. This William Hogarth was, I learnt, almost as great a painter as Mr Handel was a composer. It seems that he gave his name to certain infant foundlings, of whom I was one, and because of this he had throughout my time at the school taken a particular interest in me, and come to hear me sing often in the chapel. It was because of this gift of his name to me, this interest in me, that at twelve years old I found myself living in the servants' quarters of Mr Hogarth's fine house in Chiswick.

"I was apprenticed, along with two of my fellow foundlings, to Mr Hogarth's carriage driver, Billy Bones – Boney, as we called him. He was a sullen man, gruff in speech and gruff in appearance, with a great dislike of apprentices, and a great love of gin, spitting and cursing. All of us who worked there kept out of his way as much as possible. We were working day in, day out, in the stables, cleaning tack, grooming horses, mucking out, and cleaning and polishing Mr Hogarth's carriage.

"There was one horse I loved especially: Horace, a gentle soul, the oldest of the carriage horses. He reminded me of Friend. I would spend as much time

with him as Boney would allow.

"We all lived comfortably enough, and happily enough too, despite Boney. We were no longer at the beck and call of the school bell and our schoolmasters, nor tormented by that witch of a matron, who, with her dreaded cat-o'-nine-tails, had been the bane of our lives for so long.

"Best of all, we were always well fed and warmly clothed in Mr Hogarth's employ, and I was now earning a few pennies a week. I took great pride in that, and in my work too. I was worth something – we all were. And we were free one afternoon a week to wander the banks and meadows of the Thames near Chiswick. I loved these afternoons. I would go swimming on summer days – I was the only one of us who could, and I have to confess I took great pleasure

in that. We would eat hot pies and roasted chestnuts in winter. Nothing had ever tasted so good to me, not since Mrs Ma's tattie pie, which we had made so often together. In truth we wanted for nothing, and Mr Hogarth was kindness itself. But it was not home. Nowhere had ever been home to me but Paradise, my childhood cottage by the sea.

"As the months passed, I longed more and more to see Mrs Ma and Mr Pa again, and to discover who I was. I had a mother somewhere, and a father. Down by the Thames I would wonder about the lady selling chestnuts. Could she be my mother? I dared even ask her once if she had children of her own, but she told me to be off and to mind my own business. I decided that the only way I might ever find out was through Mrs Ma and Mr Pa. I had to find them.

"Time and again I ventured to ask my master, the kindly Mr Hogarth, if I might now after all these years be able to seek out my foster mother and father, my dear Mrs Ma and Mr Pa, but he was adamant that it could not be done, that it was not allowed by the rules of the Foundling Hospital. And furthermore, when I asked if I might ever know who my real mother and father were, it was the same answer.

"He it was who explained to me that when any mother of a foundling child gave her baby into the care of the Foundling Hospital, she left behind, to be kept safe and secret at the hospital, a token of some kind, a piece of cloth, a button, a trinket, something known only to that mother. The only way mother and child could ever be reunited was if the mother returned, recognized their token and claimed their child. It was absolutely forbidden for a foundling child ever to know who his mother was unless this occurred. He advised me, kindly but firmly, that I should not seek answers to my past, but put all that behind me, work hard at my apprenticeship and live only for my future."

"And this button in my hand..." Jonah began.

"All in good time, Jonah," the old man said, holding up his hand. "Patience. You shall know all in good time, I promise you. I still have much to tell you. After a year or so of my apprenticeship, the sad news came that Mr Montefiore had died. For me it was as if music itself had died.

"Though I did on occasion hear the sound of a distant piano or harpsichord playing somewhere deep in Mr Hogarth's house, and there was indeed a concert now and then, these days I could hear music only in snatches. Boney kept me to my work, so that if I ever heard music playing, I could never stay to listen. But I did sing, when he was not about, when no one was about. I sang to my horse, to big brown Horace, who had become my best and most trusted friend by now. He was my pride and chief joy. I kept his stable spotless, his coat shining, his hooves picked out and sound; made sure his hay was never dusty, his straw fresh. I kept my Horace happy and took great pleasure

in that, for there was gratitude and love in every look he gave me.

"I would stand beside him in his stable and sing softly to him, all the arias I remembered from the *Messiah*: 'I know that my Redeemer liveth', 'Every valley shall be exalted'. I had not forgotten a note; I remembered every word. I would rest my hand on his warm neck below his ear – it felt like warm

velvet, Jonah. His stable was now my chapel. Horace would stand so still as I sang to him, and he would listen, truly listen, Jonah.

"I was in the stable grooming Horace on the day I heard my master, Mr Hogarth, had suffered a stroke. He was gravely ill, unlikely to ever fully recover, and it was thought he could not be long for this world. I remember I walked along the riverbank in the rain so I could be alone, and I cried out loud in my sadness, because he had been a good and kind master to me. The three of them, Mr Montefiore, Mr Handel and Mr Hogarth, had been to me like three great oak trees in the parkland of my life, and I but a little sapling in their shade. And soon they would all be gone. Mrs Ma and Mr Pa I would never find again, nor my true mother and father. I felt entirely alone in the world.

"I cried again, I recall, the day I left Mr Hogarth's

house some months later, but then it was more because I was having to leave my big brown Horace behind. With Mr Hogarth ailing, there was no longer any place in his house, we were told, for apprentices from the Foundling Hospital. We were all to be sent elsewhere.

"Horace was pulling the cart that took me away from Mr Hogarth's house, away from my friends, and far out into the countryside, to be apprentice now, Boney told me, to Sir John Sullivan, a good friend of Mr Hogarth, who owned a great house and estate, and who was in urgent need of a boy apprentice in his stables. Boney also made no secret of the fact that he

was glad to be rid of me. Mr Hogarth's apprentices, and especially me, he told me, had been nothing but a trial and a nuisance to him all these years. He wanted rid of the lot of us. 'Mr Hogarth had too kind a heart, that's what I say, lettin' in all you waifs and strays,' he said. 'If no one knows your father and no one knows your mother, then you ain't worth knowin', prob'ly good for nothin'. That's what I think.'

"I did not say so, of course, but as he was speaking, I was thinking I was going to be more than glad to be rid of him also."

CHAPTER SIX

Mein Lieber Freund

THE OLD MAN SEEMED TO BE LIVING IN HIS STORY, living the moment, and for some while was silent with his thoughts. Jonah was impatient for him to continue. He wanted to know where young Nathaniel was heading, and what part the button would play.

At last the old man cleared his throat and went on.

"On the road out into the countryside," he began, "with Boney spitting and cursing all the way, Horace seemed to understand that we were coming to a parting of the ways, for he was in no hurry to arrive despite Boney's cruel whip, despite all his foul-mouthed oaths and threats. Horace took his time, plodding the rough roads and muddy lanes, and finally up a long drive through parkland where cows were grazing in large numbers, to the huge and stately mansion where I was to be working, tossing his head in his reluctance, snorting his protest. I had only a few moments to say goodbye to him, singing in his ear a last snatch of a song, resting my cheek on his warm neck for the last time, before I was led away to my little box of a room over the stable yard, where I sat on my bed and

cried, but silently so no one should hear. I was in deep despair. Horace, my last friend, was gone, and I was alone again in a strange place. I lay down, curled up on the bed, and thought of Mr Pa and Mrs Ma, of swimming in the dykes, of tickling trout, of Friend.

"It was then that I heard the sound of faraway music. Someone somewhere was playing the harpsichord, and playing it quite beautifully, a merry dancing tune that became a sad lilting melody, then suddenly a triumphant march. Such music I had never in my life heard before. The tunes mingled, played with one another merrily, spontaneously, as children do.

"I sat up, brushed my tears away, left my little room, and ran down the stairs, out of the stable yard and through the walled vegetable garden, towards the sound of the music. I found myself running along the path around to the front of the house. It was such sweet music, the notes floating out into the garden as I passed by. I found a door wide open, so I went in. I could not help myself. I knew well enough I should not intrude, that an apprentice from the stables should never set foot in the big house, but the music drew me on.

"I had never been in such a grand room; it was a place of fine carpets and tapestries, of gold-framed pictures and mirrors, of glittering chandeliers; and there at the other end of the room was a magnificent harpsichord. In front of it, on a stool piled high with scores and with a cushion atop, sat a small boy, feet dangling, so intent on his playing that he never once looked up, never noticed my approach, until I was a few paces away. When he saw me, he stopped playing at once, sprang down from his seat and ran over to me. He took me by the hand.

"'*Komm*,' he said, tugging at me impatiently. I had no choice but to go with him. He led me down the great room, out into the garden. We leapt the ditch at the bottom of the lawn and then ran off into the field, which was full of cows, the little boy pulling at my hand all the way. The cows were worried; he was giggling all the while, and when he saw the calves skipping off, he began skipping as they did, and when one of the cows farted as she ran off, he broke into cackles of raucous laughter.

"Ahead of us I saw a girl standing on the riverbank, rather older than the little boy, nearer fourteen or fifteen perhaps, my age. Still dragging me along, he ran up to her. 'Nannerl, Nannerl,' he cried. '*Ich habe einen Freund! Ein lieber Freund!*' The two of them jabbered away together excitedly. I could scarce understand a word they were saying, but it was clear they were talking about me, for the little boy was tugging still at my hand, then my coat, then my sleeve, jumping up and down with joy as if I were a great doll he had just been given. The girl was trying to calm him, but I could see from the way she spoke to him that she knew it was useless even to try.

"Then from behind me came a man's voice, shouting at me. 'Boy! You there!' Two gentlemen were hurrying towards me, the older one waving his stick, and walking, I could see, with some difficulty. 'What do you think you are doing? Who are you?' The man with the stick was more than indignant, he was angry. Nervously I told him who I was, that I had come from Mr Hogarth's house to be an apprentice in the stables of Sir John Sullivan. To my great relief he stopped waving his stick at me at once, and his entire demeanour changed. He was full of smiles, quite happy to see me.

"'So you must be Master Hogarth,' he said, shaking my hand, which took me quite by surprise. 'This is my poor friend William Hogarth's foundling boy,' he said, by way of explanation to his companion. 'He spoke of you often, young man. He thought of you very highly, which is why, when I had need of an apprentice in the stables, I asked especially for you. We have been expecting you. No one told me you had arrived.'

"By now the little boy had left my side and run up to the other gentleman, still wildly excited, still calling out as he pointed back at me. '*Er ist mein Freund, Vater. Mein lieber Freund, Vater!*' Between them all now, the two gentlemen, the girl and the little boy, there ensued an animated conversation in another language. All of them were looking at me as they spoke. I stood there quite bewildered, wondering if it was a madhouse I had come to.

"The old gentleman with the stick must have noted my confusion, and took pity on me. 'We now know well enough who you are, Master Hogarth, and so it is only fair you should know who we are. I am Sir John Sullivan, your new master, and master of Bourne Park House, where you now find yourself. And since it seems that this rather overexcited little boy has already taken a great liking to you, I should perhaps present him to you next.' The little boy was still bounding

about like a rabbit, rushing up to me and bowing low again and again as he was introduced.

"'This is Wolfgang, Wolferl we call him. He is visiting us from Austria, from Salzburg, with his father, my good friend here, Herr Mozart; and this is his sister, Maria, whom we all call Nannerl. Frau Mozart, his mother, is at present in the house. The family are staying with us here at Bourne Park for a few weeks' rest before travelling on to London, where the two children will be giving concerts.'

"'Concerts?' I asked.

"'Yes, they are much in demand, I assure you,' said my new master.

"'In demand?' I asked.

"'You must not echo me, young man.' He was speaking rather more sternly now. 'This is Wolfgang Amadeus Mozart. He is eight years old, and already famous in the world, a great musician, as indeed is his sister, Maria – Nannerl – also. They have performed all over Europe. In London they long to hear them play.'

"Wolferl was still bowing to me, still giggling, his father trying to calm and restrain him. '*Ich bin Wolfgang Amadeus Mozart, englischer Junge.*' He laughed, and grabbed my hand again. '*Wie heißt du, mein Freund? Name? Dein Name?*' I did not understand, of course.

"'He wants to know your name,' my new master explained.

"'Nathaniel Hogarth,' I said. 'I am called Nat.'

"The little boy looked up into my face, his eyes bright with affection, clinging to both my hands now. 'Nat. Nat. *Mein lieber Freund*,' he said, calmer now.

"'He says you are his friend,' explained my master, who I now noticed was standing rather bent, was waxy of complexion and did not look at all healthy. He coughed a great deal. 'You and Wolferl are well met,' he went on. 'Nannerl has just made a suggestion, which sounds to me most sensible. Wolferl, it seems, is in much need of a friend to be with him, to play with him, to guard him. He and his sister must practise every day for the concert tour. But he has been begging to have a friend to play with, a companion, shall we say. So, young man, for these few weeks the Mozart family are here, alongside your duties in the stables, you will be his playmate and guardian. He has the sweetest nature, but I should warn you that he can be a wild child, and oftentimes rather tempestuous, with little regard for his own safety, which is a great concern for his mother and father and sister. He must have someone responsible at his side at all times to keep an eye out for him. Do not let him out of your sight – is that understood?'"

CHAPTER SEVEN

Wild Child

"YOU REALLY MET MOZART?" Jonah blurted out. He knew it sounded rude, but he couldn't help himself. "You're not joking me? You knew him? My mum plays him on the piano sometimes – well, she did, anyway. Mozart. I mean, he's really famous, isn't he?"

The old man was frowning. He clearly did not like to be disbelieved, nor to be interrupted. "Indeed, he is famous, Master Trelawney," he said, clearly impatient now, "probably the most famous and certainly the greatest composer that ever lived. And yes, I had the good fortune and the honour to know him. I do not care to be doubted. This is no fanciful story I am telling you. It is as true and real as I am, as you are, as is that lucky button in your hand. There never was a luckier button. Lucky it was and lucky it is, I promise you, as you shall hear – if you would permit me to continue. Of course, if you are not interested…"

"I am, I am!" Jonah insisted.

"Very well, very well. If I recall," the old man began again, "before I was interrupted, I was telling you how

I came to assume the responsibility of looking after the young Mozart, of being the little boy's guardian. I had little time to feel pleased or displeased at my new duties. I was whisked away at once by Wolferl, and dragged down to the riverbank towards a boat that lay waiting in the reeds. It was clear what he wanted. He leapt into the boat, Nannerl jumping in after him. He stood there deliberately rocking the boat dangerously from side to side, shrieking with delight, until Nannerl grasped him firmly and pulled him down beside her, indicating to me to get in and take the oars.

"I had never in my life been in a boat before, never held an oar. I had only watched rowers out on the Thames. I had no choice but to try. Wolferl was bouncing up and down with excitement as I paddled and splashed my way down the river, trying to manage the oars as best I could. Nannerl, I was sure, could see I had never done this before and smiled her encouragement at me. She tried to keep Wolferl seated and still, but he would not do as she bade him, so the boat rocked continuously, which of course Wolferl found all the more exciting and amusing.

"Somehow, miraculously, we survived that first trip on the river, and I managed to bring us home safe and sound. But we were all soaked through from all the splashing by the time we reached the bank. We ran up through the field of cows towards the great house, little Wolferl skipping like the calves and making rude noises at the cows again, and in among the rude noises he would unaccountably burst into sudden song, conducting himself.

"Once in the house he wanted not to be parted from me for an instant, not even to go upstairs to change into dry clothes. He insisted I went with him, and that I was found dry clothing too. That was the moment I began truly to like this Wolferl. He was a sprite, a free spirit, a wild child, but generous-hearted, kind, boundless, full of laughter and endless prattle and merriment. And he loved jokes too, practical jokes, and word jokes especially – most of which I could not properly understand, of course; but I could tell well enough, from his gestures and noises, and from the obvious disapproval of everyone about him, that many were certainly not of a polite nature.

"He was no more polite when we joined with other children and workers living on the estate to play a game of what they called 'cricket'. This was a game I had never seen or heard of before, and whose rules were quite baffling to me and to little Wolferl, but a game much played, it seemed, at Bourne Park. Wolferl tired very quickly of it, unless he was batting. This part of the game he loved, and he often struck the ball with great enthusiasm and power, but as soon as he was out – and he was usually caught out quite soon – and his bat was taken away from him, he would stamp his feet in rage, and go off to lie in the long grass, where he would sulk and kick his heels. Little Wolferl could be as petulant sometimes as he was charming!"

Jonah had in mind now, as he listened, the picture of Mozart he had seen often on one of his mum's CDs, rather stiff and stern, with a neat wig. And this was the wild child the old man was describing, who giggled at farting and threw tantrums?

"When the time came for practice on the harpsichord," the old man continued, "in the great gallery hall downstairs, little Wolferl took me with him and bade me sit beside him as he played. He made it clear by showing me – understanding by now that I could not know what he was saying – what it was he wished me to do. I was to turn the pages of the music for him. I could always sing music a great deal better than I could read it, and anyway had not seen a musical score for some while now, but I did not know how to explain this to him. The notes on the page looked so unfamiliar to me. He looked into my eyes then, and seemed to understand how unsure I was of the right moment to turn the pages. For this he had a most ingenious solution. He would kick me sideways sharply with his little foot as a signal I should turn the page at once. I soon understood the message well enough.

"As he began to play, I noticed there came over this little boy a most extraordinary transformation. All that distracted feverish frolicking left him, and he lived now only for the music he was making. His little fingers danced over the keyboard. Herr Mozart – his father, and also his teacher – sat in a chair nearby, or paced up and down, mostly nodding his approval and conducting; but on occasion he would clap his hands and stop the child from his playing, to instruct and correct him, sometimes rather too harshly, I thought. Little Wolferl endured these interruptions, these admonitions, his eyes filling with tears, but was at once happy again as soon as he could resume his playing. Through it all, Frau Mozart sat at her embroidery, glowing with maternal pride.

"Wolferl insisted I was there at his side every time he played, his little kicks reminding me when to turn the page. As I did so I began to remember all that Mr Montefiore had taught me in my singing practice at the Foundling Hospital. Once learnt, it seemed, reading music is never quite forgotten. Very soon I did not need his little kicks. Wolferl sensed this, I am sure, but he tapped me every time with his foot anyway. He liked doing it, so he did it. And when Nannerl took her turn at the harpsichord, Wolferl did not allow me to turn her pages. Instead he sat himself firmly on my lap, claiming me for his own, and listened to his sister, clapping most enthusiastically when he liked her performance.

"I ate my supper beside Wolferl – he would not have it otherwise – sitting for the first time in my life in a grand dining room with my elders and betters. Wolferl would want to know what everything around him was in English. He would then translate every word into German, and have me speak it, which I found most difficult to do, and which I forgot almost immediately every time. Wolferl, though, remembered every English word I told him, testing himself and his family again and again, and was soon playing with English words, even pronouncing them backwards, and challenging me to recognize them quickly. Often I could not, and nor could anyone else, which gave him much cause for laughter. Wolferl loved merriment above all else, except music, I discovered.

"Every evening when his mother took him away to bed after supper, he complained most bitterly and would not release my hand, begging for me to go with him. His father often became angry with him at this, and Wolferl was forced to go with his mother, dragging his feet and crying. I had never known a more passionate being than this boy.

"Back in my little room over the stable I would sit on my bed, remembering all we had done together each day, the rowing, the music, the frolicking, the merriment. But I was exhausted by all this activity and always fell asleep almost at once. It was at night that the old sadness crept in. I was the happiest I had been for years, but Mrs Ma and Mr Pa and Friend and Paradise filled my dreams, so that I woke still longing for them, and thinking of the chestnut-stall lady in Chiswick who might have been my mother, and the token that would reunite us.

"Every morning I was woken early to tend to my stable work, to feed, water and groom the horses, before leading them out to grass. They were fine animals, but none were as friendly to me as Horace had been. The head groom, Mr Wickens, was a great deal jollier than Boney had been in Mr Hogarth's stables, and did not spit and curse at all. He worked us hard though. He left the care of all the horses to us, except Frederick. No one but him, I was told, was allowed to go anywhere near Fiery Frederick, as everyone called him. He was truly a giant of a creature, over seventeen hands high and jet black from head to hoof, and, according to Mr Wickens, the best carriage horse

in the entire country.

"My work in the stables being done before breakfast, I was instructed every morning to return to the house to be with little Wolferl. He was always eager to see me, eager to play in the fields and go rowing once again on the river, eager to practise his music, eager to learn more English words, and even now to try to speak always in English – imitating me. I had never in my life had a friend like this, so full of fun and affection, so enquiring, so alive to everything and everyone about him. He felt everything so powerfully, at one moment gleeful and joyous, the next plunged into the greatest sorrow and sadness. Tears and laughter followed one another with bewildering speed.

"We all lived in the glow of this small boy. He became the centre of my world at Bourne Park, as he was for everyone else there, especially Nannerl, who doted on him. She was always the only one who could calm his rages – and he fell often into rages – or his fits of wild exuberance. Her greatest joy, I could see, was to be with her little brother, to look after him, but he could not play with her as he played with me. We were boys together, best of friends at once, fast becoming inseparable. Nannerl, though, would be with us almost always, to keep an eye on us both, I thought. And I liked having her there – she was as gentle and calm as Wolferl was wild and wilful. Her English was good enough for me to understand, and like Wolferl she liked to practise speaking it with me."

Every time the old man spoke of Nannerl, it was

Valeria that Jonah had in mind. He pictured her playing with little Wolferl, making her music, smiling at him. She had become part of the story for Jonah.

"One afternoon," the old man went on, and it was a while now since Jonah had thought of him as a ghost at all, "as we were sitting quietly by the river, watching for the kingfishers that Wolferl loved to see, Nannerl asked me where my mother was. 'I have none,' I told her.

"'And your father?' she asked.

"'I have none,' I replied.

"'No sister, no brother?' Nannerl said.

"'None,' I told her.

"Wolferl turned to her. '*Er hat keine Familie?*' he said, tears in his eyes. '*Keinen Bruder?*' She shook her head. '*Du bist unser* brother, *unser* friend,' said little Wolferl, and he threw his arms round my neck. '*Mein Freund. Mein Bruder,*' he cried. I was touched to my heart by the warmth of their affection.

"Nannerl then asked me all about myself, about where I lived before I came to Bourne Park. So I told

115

her about the Foundling Hospital, my dear Mrs Ma and Mr Pa, and Paradise, my childhood home.

"It was Wolferl who asked me then, through Nannerl, the most difficult question. She translated for him. 'Wolferl asks: we have the family name of our mother and father – Mozart – and also we are given by them our first names, Wolfgang and Maria. How did you have your names if you do not have a father or a mother?'

"So I told them then how, like all the other children at the Foundling Hospital, I was given a number; that mine was 762; that each of us had a name chosen for us; and that neither Nat nor Nathaniel Hogarth was

my real name. I had no real name, for I did not know who my mother and father were. When Nannerl began to explain what I had said, to my amazement, Wolferl began to weep, his hands over his face. Then wiping his eyes he looked up at me, took my hands in his and said, '*Du bist die Nummer eins für mich, für uns, unser Freund, unser Bruder.*'

"Nannerl translated again for me. 'You are number one for me, for us, our friend, our brother.' Now I could scarcely forbear from crying myself.

"We spent long happy days together. The three of us roamed the great parklands around the house. Left almost entirely to our own devices, we went back to the house only for meals and music practice, during

which he would still tap my leg with his foot, often in rhythm with his playing. From the glances he gave me as he played I knew he still liked to have me always there beside him. Whenever I was with them the family treated me as if I was one of them, the only proper family I had known since Mrs Ma and Mr Pa. And now I had a sister; I had a brother. But still I would lie awake at night, full of longing for the one true family I never had.

"Nannerl it was who warned me one day that Wolferl was sometimes inclined to wander off, and this frightened them greatly. I knew, of course, that this was part of the reason I had been asked to be always with the little boy. Right now, she explained, little Wolferl was so attached to me, his new friend and brother, that he seemed content to stay close and remain with me and with her too; but that we should always be sure to keep him in sight, just in case he began to wander away.

"She was right. He did begin in time to stray more from my side, expecting us to follow him, and this, of course, we did. Between us we kept an eye out for him, and went running after him if he ever strayed too far. More and more, though, he liked to tease and frighten us by hiding, but he was never able to conceal himself for long. His giggling would always give him away in the end.

"All was well, until late one sunny afternoon. We were lying on our backs on the riverbank, drowsy in the humming heat, having been out all afternoon in the boat. I had closed my eyes and must have fallen asleep. Suddenly Nannerl was shaking me, shouting at me to wake. 'Gone!' she cried. 'Wolferl, *er ist weg.* Gone!'"

CHAPTER EIGHT

Hero of the Hour

"I FEARED THE WORST. There was the boat, far out in the middle of the river, one oar floating away, but no sign of Wolferl. And then I saw his head further downstream. He was floundering in the water, screaming, arms flailing, sinking, coming up, sinking again. I did not think twice – and I am no hero, I assure you – but ran down to the bank and plunged in. I felt at once the cold of the river gripping me, the weeds tugging at my legs, the flow pulling me. I struck out towards him, kicking myself free of the weeds.

"From where I found the strength I do not know, but I kept swimming, and at last managed to reach him and take hold of him. But such was his panic and

122

distress that I struggled to bring him back to the safety of the bank. I feared that in his terror he would drag us both under. Then, just when I thought all was lost, Nannerl was there to help. Together we hauled little Wolferl out of the river and onto the bank, where he sat and coughed the water out of his lungs. And when at last he had recovered, what did he do, this little friend of mine? He lifted his head, looked at us wickedly, and laughed out loud, as if it had all been the biggest, most enjoyable adventure of his life.

"He was shivering with cold and too weak to walk, so I carried him up through the field of cows and calves towards the house, Nannerl running on ahead calling for help. Even now, little Wolferl, in between his shivering and coughing and spluttering, was pointing at the cows and making again the rude noises he always made whenever he saw them.

"Everyone came running out of the house, Herr Mozart, Frau Mozart, my master, Mr Wickens, and every servant, maid and groom at Bourne Park, it seemed. Herr Mozart relieved me of the burden of little Wolferl at once, as Nannerl continued to tell them all that had happened. Crying through her smiles, Frau Mozart engulfed me in her warm embrace. Sir John ruffled my hair and told me I was a credit to the Foundling Hospital, and to the name of his dear friend William Hogarth; and everyone clapped and cheered me all the way into the house. I was the hero of the hour, and I confess I enjoyed all the attention greatly.

"I shared a hot bath with Wolferl, which shivered the cold out of us, and came downstairs hand in hand with him. The whole household was there waiting for us in the hall, applauding. Nannerl ran up the stairs to greet us, threw her arms round my neck, and whispered to me that she would love me for ever for what I had

done. Best of all, Sir John – at the request, he said, of the Mozart family – now relieved me entirely of all my stable duties and told me that, for as long as the Mozart family were staying at Bourne Park, I should live in the house with them, and sleep in little Wolferl's room; that he himself had insisted upon it."

"You saved Mozart's life?" Jonah breathed, unable in his excitement to stop himself from interrupting again. But this time the old man did not seem to mind at all. In fact he seemed positively to bask in Jonah's admiration.

"Indeed I did, Jonah," he said, smiling. "Good thing I could swim, eh? If Mr Pa had not taught me as a child, then Wolfgang Amadeus Mozart would never have composed all his glorious music, and the rest of my story – the rest of my life – could never have happened as it did.

"So," he went on, "I found myself, a foundling boy, a mere apprentice, suddenly dressed not as a stable boy, but in fine clothes and buckled shoes, living in a grand manner, and treated royally. Every day I

continued to enjoy my new-
found glory. I was the hero not
merely of the hour, but of all the
days that followed. I became,
for servant and master alike,
an honoured guest, one
of the Mozart family, best
and trusted friend of the little
boy whom everyone called '*Das
Wunderkind*', the wonder child;
and, of course, I continued to

be his page-turner too. I did wonder sometimes what
Mr Pa and Mrs Ma would think if they could see me
now, and my mother too, who remained in my mind,
in my dreams, still the woman on the chestnut stall in
Chiswick.

"During these heavenly days, the *Wunderkind* and
his sister would give concerts every evening, and I
would be there beside them at the harpsichord. They
insisted I took my bows too when the applause came,
loud and long, as it always did. Wolferl taught me to

bow low and gracefully. We would practise often out in the fields, bowing to the cows, accompanied by his usual rude noises of course. One special concert they dedicated to me, to thank me. My master invited guests from miles around. Wolferl wrote a song for Nannerl and me to sing together, having rehearsed us in our part. Nannerl then sang alone, from the *Messiah*: 'Every valley shall be exalted'. They knew this was one of my favourite arias. Can you imagine, Jonah, how happy I was that evening? Seventh heaven? No, seven hundredth heaven!

"But the time came – and of course I knew it was coming and was dreading it – for the Mozart family to leave for London, where Wolferl and Nannerl would be performing their grand concerts. Preparations for their departure were in hand, their trunks packed. I hated to contemplate their going and tried not to dwell on it, but as the day of their departure came ever closer, I could think of little else.

"On the morning they were to leave, I was there in the great hall, with everyone else from the household, waiting to bid them farewell, unsure I could hold back the tears welling inside me. So that I should not betray my emotions, I turned away to look out through the open doors and the pillars of the portico, where the carriage stood ready outside, Fiery Frederick pawing the ground, Mr Wickens standing at his head, waiting. In the hall the family were already taking their leave. Many of the household were in tears, but little Wolferl, to my great consternation, and Nannerl too, seemed quite happy to be going.

"Sir John then made a speech on behalf of us all, wishing them safe and well on their journey, and thanking them for honouring the house by their stay. Herr Mozart, his wife at his side, replied in German, rather stiffly, formally; but Frau Mozart, who seemed to think he had not said enough, spoke a few words in broken English. 'We shall not forget this place, nor your kindness, nor the river!' There was much laughter at that, of course. Then they came walking past the household towards the door, saying their farewells. I

was the last in line. But they seemed hardly to notice I was there. Indeed they passed me by without so much as a glance. Never in all my life had I felt more heartbroken.

"But just as they were leaving, little Wolferl turned. He was smiling at me, and his family were too. Then everyone burst out laughing – the Mozarts, the whole household, my master. I did not understand. It was a joke of some kind, a conspiracy, that much was obvious. But what it was I had no idea.

"Then my master, Sir John, hushed everyone, and

spoke up. 'Master Hogarth,' he said, 'you should know that two days ago Wolferl and Nannerl came to Herr and Frau Mozart and myself, and said that on no account would they play their concerts in London unless their dear friend Nat could be with them at their side. They told us that they considered him to be their brother now and best of friends, and that they would not leave this house without him. After what you have done, Herr and Frau Mozart and I were at once in agreement. So, Master Hogarth, it seems you are to go with them, be with them at their concerts – and, above all, continue to keep young Wolfgang Amadeus Mozart safe. Only when they finish their tour in this country in a year or so will you return here to continue your apprenticeship at Bourne Park.'

"Even as he was speaking, much to the joy and merriment of all who were there, Wolferl ran up to me and dragged me off through the great front door. I could scarce believe what had been said, what it really meant, nor what was happening to me. In a daze of bewilderment I found myself sitting with the family in the carriage, Wolferl on my lap, and being driven away down the drive through the parkland by Mr Wickens, with Fiery Frederick snorting and farting all the way – the beginning of a veritable symphony of vulgar sounds that accompanied us much of the journey to London, to Wolferl's great and giggling delight, and to Herr and Frau Mozart's considerable embarrassment.

"My stay with the Mozart family in London was to last for over a year. I could not count the number of concerts we played. Everywhere little Wolferl performed, the people came in their hundreds to listen, to wonder at this wonder child. He loved to perform,

loved the playing, the fame and the adulation – he
would bow again and again, laughing and giggling
all the time, in sheer delight of the moment, at the
pleasure he had given. But also, I always felt, he was
laughing at himself, because even then at that tender
age, he knew fame for what it is. He never let it touch
him. As soon as the concert and the applause and the
adulation were all over, he was himself again, a little
boy, a friend, a son, a brother. 'Fame is like a fart, Nat,'
he told me once. 'Over quickly and a bit smelly.'"

CHAPTER NINE
❯❯——❮❮

Mr King and Mrs Queen

AT THAT THE OLD MAN slapped his leg and began heaving with laughter, and then Jonah was too – he could not stop himself. It was a while before the old man had recovered sufficiently to continue his story.

"Ah, that boy," he said, shaking his head. "How he made us laugh. How wise he was, how vulgar, and what heavenly music he played, what sublime music he wrote. Through it all, throughout the whole tour, I was there with little Wolferl and Nannerl, sitting beside them, turning the pages of the music they played.

"Wolfgang was composing more and more now, every day scribbling frantically on his score, his little fingers drumming, singing the notes as he wrote with scarcely pause for thought. The strain of all this – of practising, of playing concert after concert, and of being on almost constant display – was hard for a child to endure. His health suffered, with endless coughs and fevers, and he would have to spend long days in bed recovering. I would sit with him as he composed even in bed, bring paper and pen and ink to him, listen to him humming his compositions, and Nannerl and I would sing softly to him sometimes when he was sleepy.

"Whenever he was well enough we would take the air and go walking, all of us together, through the parks of London, along the banks of the River Thames, into the great cathedrals of Westminster and St Paul's. It was during one of these walks that Wolferl said he would like to see the Foundling Hospital that by now I had told him so much about. So it was that one early morning I found myself standing outside the school, memories of the place echoing in my mind. The foundling children were filing silently out of the chapel. When I looked at little Wolferl I saw he was crying, his head on Nannerl's shoulder. His heart was so filled with pity he could scarcely bear to look at them.

"'I wish to go in,' he declared suddenly – these days he was more and more confident speaking in English. 'I wish to go to the *Kirche. Komm.*'

"Once inside, he clutched my hand tightly as we walked down the aisle. '*Keine Mutter, keinen Vater.* So *traurig*. Sad. Sad.' He looked up then and saw the organ pipes.

"'This is where Handel played,' I told him, 'where he conducted his *Messiah*, where I sang when I was little.' Nannerl translated for me, but we could see Wolferl had his mind elsewhere. He left us where we were and climbed the stairs up to the organ. We followed him, and Nannerl helped him up onto the scat.

"It was the most beautiful sound I ever heard. He was playing 'I know that my Redeemer liveth'.

"'Handel? *Ja? Ist gut?*' he cried. 'Do I play well?' He knew it by heart, note for note.

"As we walked away afterwards out of the chapel, he began speaking to me in great earnest. 'So, every child in this school wants a mother and a father. *Richtig?* Is this right?'

"'Yes,' I told him.

"'*Und du auch?*' he asked.

"Not understanding, I turned to Nannerl for help. She was always my go-between when I did not understand.

"'And this is what you wish also?' she said.

"'Yes,' I told her. 'More than anything. But it is not possible. Mr Hogarth told me so. Foundlings may not know the name of either our mother or father, or our foster parents. It is forbidden.' As Nannerl translated for Wolferl all I had said, I was plunged into a great sadness. Here at the front door of the Foundling Hospital my mother had handed me over as a babe, leaving only a token behind. There on the steps I had stood and watched Mrs Ma walk away and leave me.

"As we left the school in silence, Nannerl's hand crept into mine and she squeezed it tight. Wolferl walked on ahead, all the way home to Chelsea, hands behind his back, deep in thought.

"For days on end after this visit it rained cats and dogs, and we were kept indoors. Wolferl would, for hour after hour, sit at the harpsichord intent on his composing. When he was doing this we all knew to be silent, not to intrude. He composed feverishly, in a frenzy of excitement, humming, singing, whistling, until it was done.

"One evening he came rushing up to me, waving his score at me. He thrust the pages into my hand. '*Für dich, mein lieber Freund,*' he said, kissing me on both cheeks. '*Meine erste Symphonie.* My first symphony. I will write more, when I am older. But this is for you. Look! *Dein Name.* It has your name on the music. Look! Look!'

"I could just read his scratchy writing. *Symphonie Nummer Ein.* I could not see my name.

"Nannerl helped me to understand. 'It means Number One Symphony, Symphony Number One. Wolferl wants to say by this that you are number one to him, to all the family. You are not foundling number 762, but the brother I love, we all love, who saved my Wolferl's life. You are our number one friend.'

"'I shall play this for you, *ja?*' Wolferl cried, and
with that he ran back to the harpsichord, sat down
and played his first symphony. "*Besser mit einem
Orchester*," he said, as he played. 'Better with an
orchestra. You will see, *mein Freund. Ich werde
hundert Symphonien schreiben.* I shall write concertos,
operas, dances, marches. You will see! But this is *die
erste Symphonie, für dich*, for you.'

"As I watched him play, as I listened to the sweetness
and tenderness of the melody, my heart was filled with

joy, and with such love for him and his sister."

Any doubts Jonah might still have had about the old man's story were now gone. He was recalling his memories, not telling a tale, Jonah was quite sure of it. He could hear it in his voice, see it in his eyes. This was no fantasy; this was truth-telling. And the lucky button clasped in his hand reminded him he was not imagining any of this.

"It was a few days later," the old man went on, "upon returning home after a walk in the rain along the river at Putney – I remember the day well, as if it were yesterday, and you shall soon understand why – that we were summoned at once into the parlour. Herr and Frau Mozart were sitting side by side rather stiffly. It was clear they had something very important to say to us. I thought they would admonish us for staying out so long, and maybe for letting little Wolferl get wet – they were always worried he might catch a chill again and not be able to play his concerts. Frau Mozart called Wolferl over to her and sat him down at her feet by the fire.

"Herr Mozart spoke in German, Nannerl translating for me as he went along. 'Papa says he has news,' she told me, and her eyes lit up then with sudden excitement, her voice too. 'Papa says we are summoned to play before the king and queen at their palace.'

"At this little Wolferl leapt up from his seat by the fire with a whoop, and began cavorting about the room. 'I shall *sprechen* English like this. I shall bow thus and thus and thus,' he said, squeaking with laughter, and bowing so low with such a great and exaggerated flourish that his head almost touched the ground. 'Do I call them Herr King and Frau Queen, Mr King and Mrs Queen?'

"Then all his tomfoolery ceased quite suddenly. 'And Nat, *mein lieber Freund*, my number one friend? He must turn the pages for us. *Verstehst du doch?* I will not play otherwise, not for a king, not for anyone.' His mother and father looked at one another, unsure of what to say. '*Nicht ohne meinen Freund*. I shall not play without Nat beside me,' said little Wolferl, his chin set with determination.

"'Nor will I,' Nannerl said, grasping my hand in solidarity. Herr and Frau Mozart did not argue, because they could not and because they did not want to, I think.

"And so it was, Jonah, that this foundling boy you see before you came to perform, in a way, before King George III and the queen at the palace, with the great Wolfgang Amadeus Mozart and his sister, Nannerl. I never in my life before or since wore such fine clothes; never saw such a crowd of bejewelled lords and ladies, such shining buckles, such a gathering of powdered wigs; never set foot in such a splendid place – by comparison, Bourne Park had been but a stable.

"Little Wolferl was not in the slightest overawed, as I was, by all this grandeur. He held the stage as he always did with the greatest of ease, played his pieces with a dazzling skill, his eyes often closed in deep concentration. I turned the pages well enough, I hope, his little foot tapping my leg to remind me to focus. And then, at his insistence that they should hear it, I sang 'Every valley shall be exalted' from the *Messiah*, to his accompaniment. After it was over every person

there, the king and queen also, rose up and applauded. 'Bravo!' they cried again and again. 'Bravo!'

"The king beckoned us over to where he and the queen were sitting. The queen, I could see, was near to tears. 'Enchanting. You were enchanting. It is like a fairy story,' she said. 'To hear you playing gave me such joy. Come sit on my lap, child.'

"Little Wolferl did not hesitate, but jumped up at once, kissing her on the cheek. Everyone laughed and clapped. Then all fell silent, and out of this silence spoke little Wolferl, in his best English, with some German words sprinkled in whenever his English failed him. 'Mrs Queen,' he began.

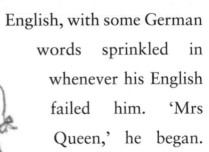

'*Bitte. Ich muss etwas fragen*, a question to ask, please.'

"'Anything, my child, anything,' said the queen.

"'My friend, Nat, *er hat keine Mutter, keinen Vater.* He is from the Foundling *Krankenhaus.* We love our mothers and fathers, *über alles.* But *mein Freund*, he does not know who his mother is; he does not know who his father is. It is not permitted for him to know who they are. The door to this question is closed. He wishes so much to find them. Frau Queen, you and Herr King rule in this land. You can open all doors that are closed. *Nein?* Can you open this door for my friend? This is my dearest wish, and his also.'

"For moments that seemed like hours the king and queen said nothing. You could have heard a pin drop, Jonah. The queen leant over then to whisper to the king. My heart beat loud in my ear; I could scarcely breathe, as we all looked to the king and the queen for a response.

"'I know the Foundling Hospital,' said the king at long last. 'A most excellent institution indeed, and one we have long sought to support.' He looked straight at me now. 'And you sang wonderfully well, young man. From the *Messiah*, was it not? I would my friend Mr Handel were still alive to have heard it and to have heard these two young people play. As to your request, Master Mozart, I think the queen would not forgive me if I denied you your dearest wish. So it is granted. I will do what I can.'

"At this the hall filled with clapping again. Wolferl kissed the queen once more, sprang down and ran to me. Then, bowing low, all three of us together – we had practised this before in our lodgings –backed away out of the room, the applause ringing in our ears.

"The next day, by special messenger, there arrived at our house in Chelsea a small package on which was written: By command of His Majesty King George III. Wolferl gave it to me at once to open. Inside was a cardboard box, and in the box a folded letter, and, enfolded in the letter, the brass button you hold now in your hand, Jonah."

"This is it?" Jonah asked, gazing down at the button in his palm. "This is the actual one?"

"It is," replied the old man.

"But was it really a lucky button?" Jonah asked him. "Did you see Mrs Ma and Mr Pa again? Did you find your mother and your father?"

"Life, Jonah," said the old man, "as you know as well as I, is not a fairy tale. We can never have all we wish for. Sadness we cannot avoid, but we can also know great joy. I could tell you a fairy tale, or I could tell you the truth. Truth or fairy tale; tell me Jonah, which would you like?"

CHAPTER TEN

Truth or Fairy Tale?

JONAH FOUND HIMSELF turning the button over and over in his hand. He closed his eyes and hoped.

"Truth," Jonah replied.

"Very well, then, you shall hear the truth," the old man said. "The button, as you have guessed, was my mother's token. Upon reading the letter that came with it, I found the date of my birth, and my real name, Daniel Morley, son of Bethany, of 75 Lupin Street in Southwark. We went at once, that very same morning, all of us together, to find the room where she lived in Southwark.

It was above the baker's shop, we discovered, where she had once worked. But she was no longer there, the baker's wife told us, and no longer alive either.

"I had such strange thoughts when I first heard this dreadful news. Yet, I reasoned, to know such news was better than not to know. And I found I was sad that the lady selling chestnuts in Chiswick was not my mother, but I was glad my mother had such a beautiful name. Bethany, Bethany. My mother, Bethany. We learnt from the baker's wife that she had been barely sixteen years old, and had loved her baby, she said, as much as any mother that ever lived. She went off with him one day in tears, saying her family would never have her home again with the child; that she could not feed and care for him on her own. He would have a better chance to survive if she took him to the Foundling Hospital. It would not be for ever, she said, and she would go back and reclaim him when she was older. That was the last time the baker's wife saw her. She heard she had died a year or so later, but where she was buried she did not know.

"When I asked about my father, the baker's wife said she saw him only once, just after I had been born. He was a soldier. She remembered his red coat and his bright buttons, just like my token. She thought he went to fight abroad and, so far as was known, had never returned.

"All this news left me numb, not saddened by grief, for I had never known her or him, but empty of all feeling, suddenly orphaned and alone in the world.

"But Herr and Frau Mozart were even more anxious now, as were dear Wolferl and dear Nannerl, to help me further, and would not leave it there. I told them I had one more hope left: to find Mrs Ma and Mr Pa. Frau Mozart it was who decided what should be done, and how it should be done too. The more I came to know her, the more I realized that, quiet and retiring as she might often seem, she was the guiding light of the family. At her suggestion, we went again to the Foundling Hospital, where once they realized who we were, they received us with the greatest courtesy.

"At Wolferl's side, in the glow of his fame, I found

I was treated now with rather more respect than I had received before as a small child. Frau Mozart told them that Wolferl would play on the organ in the chapel for the children, if they would like it, which of course they did. The foundling children sat in rapt attention throughout, the schoolmasters too. The witch of a matron was there, but I stared her down, and that gave me much pleasure.

"As we left the chapel, Frau Mozart asked the master of the Foundling Hospital in her best English: 'I have a favour to ask for our dear friend Nat, who was a child here as you know. We wish to discover, sir, where we might find his foster mother and father, and their names also. They are his only family, sir."

"The master hesitated for a moment, his eyes darting nervously.

"'Where they live, that is all we wish to know. Or...' Frau Mozart went on, not troubling now to disguise the threat in her voice, 'or we could ask our friend, the king.'

"With the address in my hand we all travelled the

very next day by coach to the coast of Essex, through the flatlands and marshes, along the familiar dykes where moorhens swam among the bulrushes, all the way to the little village of Bradwell. As soon as I saw the church tower rising through the trees, I knew where I was. From there I knew my way down the lane to Paradise Cottage. I was home at last. Smoke

rose from the chimney. There were voices inside, and the smell of cooking, of pastry, of tattie pie. I knocked on the door.

"Thus was I reunited with my dear Mrs Ma and Mr Pa. There never was a gladder reunion; and Friend was there in the orchard, older, but so were we all. My lucky button was doing its work. I had found my beloved family again.

"But my joy was to be short-lived, for within a few months the Mozart family left for France, and I returned to my apprenticeship at Bourne Park. We three children swore we would meet again and soon; that we would be friends for ever. Though I was saddened beyond words at our parting, the gift of their friendship stayed with me in my heart for ever. Through my lucky button, which I could never have discovered without them, they had given me the greatest gift imaginable: the knowledge of who I was, from where and from whom I came, and my dear home and family.

"Both Wolferl and Nannerl wrote letters to which I always replied. In time, though, as I grew older, now living and working on the farm with Mrs Ma and Mr Pa, having finished my apprenticeship at Bourne Park, the letters became less frequent. But a day never went by that I did not think of them, nor did I doubt for a moment that they still loved me as much as I loved them. I followed Wolferl's rise and rise, heard his music played often, whenever I could. I hummed and sang it too, to myself and to the moorhens, to the sheep, to

Friend, as I walked the fields around Bradwell, to Mrs Ma and Mr Pa to whom I remained devoted all their long lives.

"I remained devoted to music all my life too – this great and lucky gift that between them Mrs Ma and Mr Montefiore, and Mr Handel and chiefly Wolferl and Nannerl had given me – becoming choirmaster in the end at the Foundling Hospital, where I might not always have been happy as a child, but to which I owed so much. Without that old witch of a matron, it was a much happier place anyway.

"When I heard of Wolferl's early death, I was overwhelmed with sadness. I travelled to Austria to see Nannerl, and stood with her in silence, hand in hand, in the place where we thought he had been buried, in an unknown common grave. To see her and be with her was the greatest joy, but without Wolferl there with us, the blithe spirit of both our lives, we were often too sad to speak.

"We wrote to one another for many years, but never met again. When the letters stopped coming, I knew she was gone. It was my turn then. I was buried in the

chapel of the Foundling Hospital, and they brought
me here and laid me in the crypt when they moved the
school, nearly a hundred years ago now. I like it here. I
can hear the children sing and laugh. They laugh these
days more than we ever did, and that is good." He
stood up to leave. "It has done me good to tell my
story. I knew you would understand. You know about

sadness; you know about joy, and music."

"Your lucky button," Jonah said, offering it back to him.

"Keep it," the old man told him. "You have more need of it than I. I hope it will be as lucky for you as it was for me. Consider it as thanks for giving me a chance to tell my story. And think of me sometimes, and Wolferl and Nannerl, and Mrs Ma and Mr Pa. We only live on in our stories."

He walked away from him and vanished into the darkness at the back of the chapel.

Jonah was woken by someone shaking his shoulder. Mrs Rainer was bending over him. He found himself stretched out on the pew. He sat up, bewildered.

"You didn't come back to rehearsals, Jonah. I was worried. Are you all right?"

"Fine," Jonah told her. "I'm fine."

She insisted on taking him back to the school nurse, who took his temperature and his pulse just to make sure he was as fine as he said he was. She made him lie down for an hour, so she could keep an eye on him. He was happy to be left alone.

He spent the rest of the day in a state of bewilderment, drifting from lesson to lesson, unable to concentrate on maths or French or history. He kept feeling for the button in his pocket to reassure himself that all he had seen and heard had not been a dream.

At the end of the school day, he was walking home, still in a daze, when he found he was not alone. Valeria was there beside him. They walked on together in silence for a while, Valeria pushing her bike. He longed to talk to her, to tell her everything that had happened.

He sensed that she would believe him. But no words would come out.

"I will see you tomorrow then, Jonah?"

"Yes," he said. "Bye."

"Bye. And I have wanted to say that you sing very well," she said. Then off she went on her bike.

One day, Jonah thought, I will tell you about everything that happened in the chapel. And you will be the only one in the world I will tell.

The swallows were still flying as he walked home, gripping his lucky button tight all the way. Only then did it occur to him that the luck was working already. Valeria had spoken to him! He knew now for sure that she was a true friend.

There were rabbits grazing at the edge of the woods. Coocoo was up on the chimney waiting for him. Jonah was opening the front door, stepping into his other world, when he heard music playing from the sitting room. The piano. His mum must be playing the piano again! He knew the music. He had heard it before somewhere; he was sure of it.

His mum did not hear him as he came in. She was too intent on her playing. He stood there listening, marvelling, the lucky button warm in his hand. It was some while before she felt him there, and looked up.

"Hello, Jonah," she said cheerily. "Look at me, playing again. Don't know what came over me. I was looking at the piano, and it was as if it spoke to me. 'Play me,' it said. 'I'm no use if you don't play me.' And I said right back, 'And I'm no use if I don't play you.' So here we are. And here you are!" She was beaming up at him, holding out her hand and grasping his arm. "I feel so much better for playing some music, Jonah. You can't imagine. Did you like it? Mozart. I'm a bit out of practice, a bit rusty, but Mozart won't mind. It's his Symphony No. 1. He wrote it when he was only eight, you know. How was school? Good day? How did rehearsals go? I'm coming to your play, I've decided. I've got to get out and about more, like you said. So I'll be there at your *Lord of the Flies* show. Three weeks' time, isn't it? It had better be good!"

She was there too, her first proper trip out of

the house for over two years. Jonah wheeled her all the way there and back. "That girl who played the clarinet," she said to him as they paused by the gate to watch the swallows, "she was wonderful. But your song was the best, Jonah. Just the best. I'm so proud."

Jonah squeezed the lucky button deep inside his pocket. "Thanks," he whispered, louder than he meant to.

"Thanks, Jonah? Why are you thanking me? I reckon it's me who should thank you. We have music and we have each other. That's a lot to be thankful for."

MICHAEL MORPURGO is one of the greatest storytellers for children writing today. He has won numerous major literary awards, including the Nestlé Children's Book Prize, the Whitbread Children's Book Award and the Writers' Guild Award. Author of more than a hundred books, including retellings of classics such as *Hansel and Gretel* and *The Pied Piper of Hamelin*, Michael was also Children's Laureate from 2003 to 2005. His books have been translated around the world, and his hugely popular novel *War Horse* was adapted into a critically acclaimed stage play and film. He also founded the charity "Farms for City Children" with his wife Clare, for which he was awarded an MBE.

MICHAEL FOREMAN is one of the world's leading illustrators. He has won several major awards, including the Kate Greenaway Medal twice. Born in Sussex, Michael was inspired by the illustrated magazines in the village shop that his mother ran, and at fifteen he began to study art. He has illustrated more than 300 books by authors such as Shakespeare, the Brothers Grimm and Charles Dickens, and has also written many of his own, including the award-winning classic *War Boy*. Michael has previously collaborated with Michael Morpurgo on books including *The Mozart Question* and *Beowulf*.

ABOUT THIS STORY AND THE FOUNDLING MUSEUM

Although Nathaniel's story is fictional, it was inspired by real people and events. The Foundling Hospital was a real place opened by Thomas Coram in 1741, and William Hogarth and George Frideric Handel were early supporters. Handel first conducted the Messiah *in the chapel in 1750. Babies taken to the Hospital were looked after by foster families, before returning to be educated until they took up apprenticeships or entered domestic or military service.*

If you would like to discover more about the Foundling Hospital and the children who grew up there, a visit to the Foundling Museum is the best place to start. A short walk from the British Museum and built on the site of the original Hospital, which continues today as the charity Coram, we tell the fascinating story of the UK's first children's charity and first public art gallery through displays, exhibitions and fun activities.

The Museum contains many features saved from the original Hospital building, including pews and decorations from the Chapel. You can also see paintings and sculptures by artists such as William Hogarth and Thomas Gainsborough; items relating to the life and work of composer George Frideric Handel, including the *Messiah* score he gave to the Hospital; and objects relating to the lives of the foundling children. Among these are the eighteenth-century "tokens", the small everyday objects that mothers left with their

babies as a means of identification, should they ever return to claim their child. The tokens are extraordinarily moving objects that range from coins, gambling tokens and jewellery, to good luck charms, tickets and buttons.

One of the ways in which creative people continue the legacy established by Hogarth and Handel, is through our Fellowship programme. Foundling Fellows are remarkable and inspiring people who bring the Hospital's history to life with projects that celebrate the power of the arts to change lives. Charles Dickens was a supporter of the Foundling Hospital in the nineteenth century and writers are an important part of the Fellowship. Michael Morpurgo became a Foundling Fellow in 2012 and we are hugely proud that this association has resulted in a story as magical and moving as *Lucky Button*.

Caro Howell, Director, The Foundling Museum
foundlingmuseum.org.uk